D0458719

YOUR MOST OBEDIENT SERVANT

YOUR MOST OBEDIENT SERVANT

JAMES THORNTON

Cook to the Duke of Wellington

With an Introduction by
Elizabeth Longford

First published in Great Britain 1985 by
Webb & Bower (Publishers) Limited
9 Colleton Crescent, Exeter, Devon EX2 4BY

Designed by Malcolm Couch
Production by Nick Facer

British Library Cataloguing in Publication Data

Thornton, James
Your most obedient servant : cook to the Duke of Wellington.
1. Wellington, Arthur Wellesley, *Duke of*
2. Great Britain. *Army* —Biography 3. Generals —Great Britain—Biography
I. Title
941.07'092'4 DA68.12.W4

ISBN 0-86350-089-7

Typeset in Great Britain by P&M Typesetting Ltd., Exeter, Devon
Printed and bound in Great Britain

Contents

Daily life with Wellington's army, from J.H. Pyne's *Camp Scenes*, 1803.

Introduction by Elizabeth Longford

THE DISCOVERY OF THIS DOCUMENT, consisting as it does of a long series of replies by Wellington's cook to a questionnaire, is doubly exciting. First for its intrinsic interest, second for the hopes such a discovery always raises of future finds. Like all historians I have a favourite dream of suddenly locating in some dusty trunk that other half of a long lost correspondence, or those memoirs that are *said* though never *proved* to have been burnt. But this questionnaire addressed to and answered by Wellington's cook is in a category of its own.

No one seems to have heard of it until now. Yet its authenticity is not in doubt. It is the work of a man who

Lord Frederick Fitzclarence, Lieutenant-Governor of Portsmouth.

had served Wellington during well over half the Peninsular War and for virtually the whole of his Waterloo campaign. Wellington was still alive when Thornton's employer, Lord Frederick Fitzclarence, Lieutenant-Governor of Portsmouth, questioned him during the winter of 1851-2. Wellington died at Walmer Castle in September 1852, so, if Thornton had given any dubious or unconvincing replies, Fitzclarence could conceivably have checked up with the Duke in person.

Moreover, Frederick Fitzclarence himself was a man of some consequence. A younger son of the Duke of Clarence, afterwards King William IV, and of the actress Mrs Jordan, Lord Frederick and his numerous brothers and sisters were known in polite society as *les bâtards*. He became Lieutenant-Governor of Portsmouth in succession to Wellington's brother-in-law 'good old Sir Hercules Pakenham', as the Portsmouth records call him. We may perhaps see in this Pakenham–Fitzclarence connection some explanation of Thornton's employment. Fitzclarence proved an innovator, bringing benefits to the soldiers, garrison and citizens of Portsmouth under his command through his lavish personal spending and 'royal' influence. He is still remembered in the city for his construction of a 'noble' beach promenade called after him. His biographer writes: 'The hospitality of Fitzclarence was proverbial', which suggests that Thornton had become no mean cook.

Fitzclarence had already employed Thornton for five years and thought the world of him. ('I can not give him *too* good a character.') As I shall have to show at the conclusion of these introductory remarks, the Duke was probably unable to give Thornton such a superlative 'character' when he finally left the ducal service, in England, at the beginning of 1821. Nevertheless, Thornton must have greatly pleased Wellington in the Peninsula, for Sir Colin Campbell was again to summon him from London, this time to Brussels before Waterloo. Campbell's judgment was thoroughly trusted by Wellington. He had picked him out as a very young officer in India, first spotting him 'in the air', as he was toppled from a scaling ladder at the siege of Ahmednuggur. When Sir Arthur Wellesley (as Wellington still was) sailed to Portugal for the second time, in 1809, it was Colin Campbell who, as his ADC, had a characteristic tale of Wellesley's unflapability during a perilous Atlantic storm. Summoned by the agitated captain to put on his boots and come on deck, Wellesley replied that he could swim better without boots and would remain below.

James Thornton's story will profit from a brief summary of the Peninsular War, before the detailed consideration of his replies to questions.

After the abortive British attempt of 1808–9 to liberate the Iberian Peninsula from Napoleon's armies, which culminated in the disaster of Corunna, Wellesley was sent out again in April 1809 with the order to sweep the French from Portugal and Spain also, in so far as he would deem that practicable. A similar order was being given by Napoleon to his generals: to drive 'the hideous leopard' (England) into the sea.

Opposite:

Two of Wellington's most trusted comrades-in-arms: Major-General Sir Colin Campbell (left), one of the aides-de-camp who survived Waterloo, and Major-General Sir Frederick Ponsonby who was hideously wounded at Waterloo but, unlike many of his fellow officers, was found alive after the battle.

Austrian camp scene in 1814.

The two years between 1809 and 1811, when Thornton arrived, were sometimes gloriously, sometimes painfully eventful. Wellesley called the capture of Oporto his 'greatest adventure'; after the victory of Talavera in Spain he was created Viscount Wellington of Talavera; with troops severely handicapped by lack of supplies and money, he was forced to evacuate Spain and retreat into his lines of Torres Vedras for the winter of 1810–11, after winning an unexpected victory at Busaco on the way. From his Portuguese 'Lines', the French under Marshal Massena were unable to oust him. They themselves made a dash back into Spain in March 1811. With a now fit army, Wellington felt that he could again advance, after first capturing the keys of Spain: the two border fortresses of Ciudad Rodrigo and Badajoz. Having besieged the former, he wrote cautiously in August 1811: 'we have certainly altered the nature of the war in Spain; it has become, to a certain degree, offensive on our part'.

It was in this same August 1811 that Colin Campbell engaged Thornton in London as Wellington's cook. Summer fevers were already rampant among the troops and Wellington himself was distinctly off-colour for a fortnight. His daily routine – up at 6am, 6–9 writing, breakfast, visits of heads of all departments till 3pm, riding 3–6, dinner, 9–12 writing – this spartan regime needed temporarily modifying. Perhaps a new cook was to be one element in a return to robust health.

By the autumn Rodrigo had still not been captured; indeed the new French commander, Marshal Marmont, relieved and revictualled it in late September. The Allied army went into cantonments (billets) from 1 October to 1 December.

Thornton arrived at Freineda, Wellington's winter

headquarters, near the beginning of this recuperative period, in good time to see Ciudad Rodrigo captured on 19 January 1812 and Badajoz, after appalling sufferings and atrocities, on 6 April. Wellington became a British earl, Portuguese Duque de Ciudad Rodrigo and a Grandee of Spain. These two cruel but memorable sieges were followed up on 22 July by the victory of Salamanca, leading directly to Wellington's triumphal entry into Madrid in August. He was created a marquess. It seemed possible that the Allies might capture that autumn the threatening fortress of Burgos in Old Castile, from whose towers the jagged slate-blue beginnings of the Pyrenees were distantly visible. They might even be in Paris for Christmas. But fate was against them. Grimly Burgos held out and Wellington's despondent army once more retreated for the winter to their old cantonments at Freineda, where Thornton had first joined them the year before.

Next year, 1813, was a very different story. The campaign began in May. With superb skill, Wellington got his whole army across the River Ebro by June and, having marched four hundred miles in forty days, on the 21st captured not only Vittoria but also the mass of abandoned French baggage and booty. There followed the sieges of San Sebastián and Pamplona and the battles of the Pyrenees, by which Wellington's armies inexorably crossed the river lines of France – Bidassoa, Nive, Nivelles,

Thomas Heaphy's painting of the Duke of Welling

ving orders to his generals before a battle.

Adour, Joyeuse, Bidouse and Gave d'Oloron. These victories culminated in the battle of Toulouse on Easter Sunday, 10 April 1814, narrowly won by Wellington seven days *after* Napoleon had abdicated in Paris. The ex-emperor agreed to go into exile on lovely Elba with a handsome pension of six million livres. Wellington became a duke. For Thornton as for Wellington it was the end of the Peninsular War. Thornton was naturally replaced by French chefs when the Duke was appointed British Ambassador to the Court of the Tuilleries in 1814. But Napoleon's dramatic return to France in 1815 and his Hundred Days of freedom were to lead to Thornton's own recall, so to speak, to the 'kitchen colours'.

Wellington's opinion of his wartime hospitality and Thornton's cooking was modest rather than glowing. In comparing the dinners given by himself and his outstanding generals, he once said: 'Cole gives the best dinners in the army; Hill the next best; mine are no great things; Beresford's and Picton's are very bad indeed!' In other words Wellington had no ambition to employ a world-famous chef such as Napoleon's Monsieur Dunand or Talleyrand's Monsieur Carême who would be creating his fantastic *pièces montées*, temples, idols, harps, castles, caryatids – while Wellington was ambassador in Paris. If Napoleon had said an army 'marches on its stomach', that was no reason for Wellington to believe it to be true of a commander-in-chief's stomach also.

Of course it is possible that Wellington's deprecatory remarks about his dinners were aimed at Thornton's predecessor rather than Thornton himself. The story, as first told by Edward Fraser in 1913, relates to '*Lord* Wellington's' dinner, and Wellesley had become a lord after Talavera in July 1810, a year before Thornton came

Lord Edward Somerset, one of Wellington's staff in the Peninsular Campaign.

Lord Henry Paget, Earl of Uxbridge and 1st Marquess of Anglesey, the commander of Sir John Moore's cavalry at Corunna. In 1809 he caused a scandal by eloping with Wellington's sister-in-law.

out. Nevertheless, the anecdote is undoubtedly meant to suggest that Wellington's Peninsular dinners were never 'great things'. That was not the case with his drinks. He loved his cup of tea, sending to London for some 'black tea' after Oporto and providing excellent champagne (also sent out from London) and claret at his dinner-parties.

Thornton's birth in Bryanston Street sounds fairly humble, though not so humble as the great Carême's, who was turned out by his father either to starve or survive in the streets of revolutionary Paris. The Bryanston Street district was not so fashionable as it was to become in the nineteenth century. (There was no Marble Arch in front of it until very many years later.) But it was an area favoured by French *émigrés*, some of whom Wellington probably knew since they had been settled there by his great friend Lord Buckingham. Moreover, Arthur Wellesley's married life had begun at nearby 11 Harley Street, also in the parish of St Marylebone. Indeed, he himself may have put Colin Campbell on to Thornton, who in turn may have been connected with the French community in London. The names of the men to whom Thornton had been apprenticed lend some support to this theory.

After his engagement by Campbell, Thornton lost no time in going out to join Wellington; the fact that he set sail from Portsmouth may have stimulated the Lieutenant-Governor's later interest. In regard to Thornton's march from Lisbon to Wellington's HQ, there are several points to be noted. First, he covered twenty miles a day though the average was only fifteen miles a day for the Peninsular armies. Thornton was lucky to be riding with a detachment of cavalry. Second, the desolation of the Portuguese villages, indelibly printed on Thornton's mind, was in fact the greatest mistake made by the French.

Thornton was witnessing the results of the French 'system' of requisitioning by which they would live off the country, ransacking and denuding all occupied territory. Partly in revenge for this treatment, the Portuguese *ordenanza* (armed peasants) and Spanish guerrillas organized themselves to waylay and murder any isolated Frenchman they could find and thereby to support Wellington. Payment by the British for all food and supplies was officially their much appreciated 'system'. Sometimes, however, it was put in jeopardy by the meanness of the home government.

'Frenada' (Freineda), Wellington's HQ during two winters, 1811–12 and 1812–13, must have struck Thornton as a singularly unassuming background against which to see the army's hero for the first time. Its market-place was tiny even for a Portuguese village, only the little church being remarkable for the seemingly perpetual activity of its bell. Wellington's house was up some steps opposite the church. With only the young son of Lord Enniskillen's cook and a scullery maid to assist him, Thornton could not be expected at this stage to produce 'great dinners'. His remark about 'no regular luncheons' rings true. Wellington's staff noticed that in days of hard riding he occasionally carried a crust and a hard-boiled egg in his pocket, no more. After the war was over (1814), British officers riding through France would carry hard-boiled eggs in their pistol holsters.

Thornton's recollections of Wellington's personal staff are surprisingly accurate, considering that he was looking back from forty years on. He may of course have served and met some of them in the years between. In those days (as also today in the remaining great houses) servants were recommended and passed on from one to another or

Spanish light infantrymen *c.* 1805.

blackballed and dropped. In order of Thornton's list, Lord Fitzroy Somerset (a scion of the great Beaufort family) was married to Wellington's niece Emily Wellesley-Pole and was to lose his right arm at Waterloo. Wellington always praised him for his exceptional truthfulness and exactness in carrying out orders. Alas, after 1852 the Duke was no longer alive to direct Fitzroy. Created Lord Raglan, he replaced Wellington as Commander-in-Chief and met his 'Waterloo' in the Crimea, where he died of a broken heart.

Major Alexander Gordon, destined to lose his leg and life at Waterloo, was a younger brother of the 4th Earl of Aberdeen. His monument was restored by the family in 1965, the 150th anniversary of the battle. Major Burgh, later Sir Ulysses Burgh and later still Lord Downes, typified the kind of young aristocrat whom Wellington delighted to have in his 'military family', as he called his personal staff.

Colin Campbell's connection with Wellington was long and honourable, as mentioned above. He was to become Sir Colin Campbell, Governor of Ceylon.

Lord March, eldest son of Wellington's friend the Duke of Richmond, was soon to serve as ADC to the Prince of Orange in the Waterloo campaign. Lord March's mother gave the famous Waterloo Ball; his sisters, the young Lennox ladies, were entertained by Wellington at cricket matches and family 'romps' before the battle, while his father and teenage brother turned up together on the battlefield. Wellington told them both to go home, the one being too old, the other too young for fighting, but neither obeyed the C-in-C's orders.

Captain 'Freemantle' (Fremantle) came of a distinguished Buckinghamshire family who later were to acquire the Cottesloe peerage. He attended Wellington (along with another Lennox) in his hectic carriage drive to the Congress of Vienna. Neither Fremantle nor Lennox undressed at the inns where they stayed on the way. Wellington, who was popularly supposed to have slept in his clothes throughout the Peninsular War, seems to have had enough of it by 1815; he changed into his nightshirt, appearing each morning immaculate before his two rumpled ADCs.

General Miguel de Alava, Wellington's Spanish liaison officer throughout the war, remained his friend at Stratfield Saye House during the years of peace. He was responsible for the neatest summary of the Duke's spartan habits. 'When Alava travelled with the Duke', remembered a friend, 'and asked him what o'clock he would start, he usually said, "at daylight"; and to the question what they would find for dinner, the usual answer was "*cold meat*"!' Alava came to dread those three words, *daylight* and *cold meat*, as he dreaded nothing else during the campaign!

As regards the adjutant and quartermaster-generals, Wellington's highly valued brother-in-law, Edward (Ned) Pakenham, had become his assistant adjutant-general in 1809; the best of his quartermaster-generals was Sir George Murray, who once joked that the British army would make war in Spain and Portugal to the last pound of beef and mutton.

A regular and popular guest at Wellington's table was the young Prince of Orange, known as 'Slender Billy' because of his long thin neck. The 'Baron Something' whom Thornton remembers as the Prince's tutor was in

Overleaf:
General Miguel Ricardo de Alava, Wellington's Spanish liaison officer in the Peninsular Campaign.

fact the very distinguished Baron Jean de Constant Rebecque, thanks to whose daring and initiative on 15 June 1815 a literal walk-over at Quatre Bras was denied to Napoleon's Marshal Ney.

Unfortunately social etiquette would have inhibited the Lieutenant-Governor of Portsmouth from asking James Thornton questions about Wellington's personal relations with his staff. However, we have various reports from other sources, some of them contradictory. Wellington did prefer to have 'gilded' youth on his personal staff, as the above list implies. They were the sons of his friends or relations and were his wartime 'family' in a real sense. On the other hand, there had to be reliability beneath the gilding. His nephew William Wellesley-Pole was sent packing when he misbehaved and took French leave; 'Wicked William', as he was called in the family, lived to vote against his uncle the Duke at the great Reform Bill debate.

It has sometimes been said that conversation was difficult at Wellington's table, 'the Peer', as they called him, seldom taking his generals into his confidence and occasionally 'humbugging' (deceiving) them deliberately about his strategy, to prevent leaks. But as the war progressed he seems to have become a more genial host, discussing many subjects from the Poor Law to Catholic Emancipation. His dinners also tended to last longer. Perhaps Thornton's cooking had been partly responsible for a higher general standard.

When Thornton gets on to particular battles, his accuracy is on the whole most commendable: Salamanca for a start. His memory of Wellington munching a cold chicken leg in the farmyard before the action was a true and picturesque part of that great day. It was at that moment that Wellington received the crucial news that Marshal Marmont had dangerously extended his line. Mounting his charger, Wellington galloped off across the tawny dust bowls or stony hillocks to give the essential order to his brother-in-law: 'Ned, d'ye see those fellows on the hill? Throw your division into column; at them and drive them to the devil.' This was Ned Pakenham's finest hour, when his prompt manoeuvre led to the defeat of '40,000 Frenchmen in 40 minutes'. Incidentally, Thornton was right in saying that he did *not* cook Wellington's dinner on the 'day' of Salamanca; Fitzclarence exaggerated in deducing from the questionnaire that Thornton had cooked the dinner after every single great action. (Fitzclarence's error was later repeated by Thornton in a letter to *The Times*. See p.49.)

Captain Canning, the ADC, who found Thornton and his 'kitchen furniture' on the day after Salamanca waiting beside the River Tormes and directed him forward, was to lose his life like so many others at Waterloo.

The triumphal entry into Madrid was no less thrilling than it appeared in James Thornton's recollection. The 'King' in whose palace Wellington lunched was King Joseph Bonaparte, Napoleon's brother, the legitimate Spanish King Ferdinand being Napoleon's prisoner. It was on this occasion that the inimitable Goya seized a canvas bearing Joseph's likeness and painted it out with a celebrated equestrian portrait of Wellington. Thornton's impression that the famous 'Wellington boots' were kissed as well as everything else by the madly excited populace is a pleasant addition to our knowledge.

Wellington's dress at Salamanca, on which Thornton was questioned, may well have been as he described it. His battle-dress was always plain and *civilian*, never a military

Wellington's dressing case which accompanied him on his campaigns.

uniform except at formal reviews. It varied to some extent. As the Peninsular years passed, Wellington had the skirts of his blue 'frocks' cut shorter for smartness' sake; his trousers could be grey or pepper-and-salt ('mixed coloured') or white buckskin breeches; his *white* stock differed from the regulation black one; and his 'plain' cocked hat, worn fore and aft, had no white cock's feathers, though at Waterloo the four cockades of his British, Spanish, Portuguese and Dutch forces were proudly worn by him. There is a print of Wellington and his generals preparing to cross the River Bidassoa into France. All except Wellington and one other are wearing white plumes in their hats, the 'other' being altogether hatless, having apparently taken a tumble off his horse. Wellington occasionally wore a low top-hat ('round hat') and in the stormy Pyrenees he chose a white Spanish cloak taken from a French dragoon as well as an oilskin over his small cocked hat. This he pulled well down over his aristocratic nose – but not so far down that his troops could not recognize his galloping figure at the battle of Sorauren and shout, 'Nosey! Nosey!'. His other nickname was 'the Beau' because he was always so meticulously, though plainly, turned out.

Wellington's two balls given in Madrid were grander than usual, being held in a capital city with a palace ballroom. He could nonetheless summon up grandeur whenever the occasion demanded. For instance, a grand dinner and ball given at Ciudad Rodrigo in March 1813 in honour of Sir Lowry Cole, who was invested with the Order of the Bath, was furnished with silver, fruit, flowers and delicacies brought from far and near in Portugal and decorated with yellow satin hangings. (It strikes me that Wellington's passion for yellow silk wallpapers at Apsley

Goya's portrait of Wellington painted in Madrid in 1812. The painting covers an earlier one by the artist of King Joseph, whose shadow can be seen behind the Duke's head.

House after the war – much criticized by his friends – derived from nostalgic memories of his wartime gaieties.)

Officers' balls were often muted affairs, since they could not always afford more than lemonade and cakes for refreshments, while a shortage of ladies forced them to partner each other. At one dance the solitary girl present waltzed until she dropped. Wellington's soldiers would enjoy chestnut suppers, joining in local *boleros* and *fandangos*, some of them being bewitched, others shocked, by the wriggling 'bottoms' of the local belles.

As far as food and service were concerned, it was the universal custom to put almost all the eatables on the table at once, with never more than 'two courses'. Monsieur Carême, the patron saint of chefs, was to invent the elaborate service of eight or more separate courses. A typical example of a dinner-party given by one of Wellington's generals in the autumn of 1813 consisted of, *first course*: roasts, steaks, chicken, ham; *second course*:

partridges, stewed apple tart, mushrooms, grapes. Thornton would have gone marketing in the summer to provide Wellington's table with green vegetables and tomatoes.

One surprising fact about the Fitzclarence questionnaire is that he asked Thornton next to nothing about the actual food he cooked. I can think of no reason but the obvious one: Wellington's regular dinners were so ordinary that there was really nothing to discuss. Beef, mutton, potatoes; potatoes, mutton, beef.

In discussing the disgraceful, indisciplined, drunken retreat from Burgos, Fitzclarence has another curious omission. Nothing is asked or reported about Wellington's efforts to restore the order and morale of his army; the arrests and floggings, even the execution of those soldiers who killed the Spanish peasants' livestock and murdered the peasants themselves. Again, there can be only one explanation: tact and good taste. No one wanted to remember the hell that Wellington and his army went through after Burgos. And after all, Portsmouth was a great naval base and Fitzclarence would have been hardened to accounts of naval floggings. There is a story of Wellington's connection by marriage, Admiral Pakenham, sailing into Portsmouth and being questioned about the state of his crew. He replied, 'Oh, I have left them all to a man, the merriest fellows in the world. I flogged seventeen of them, and they are happy it is over, and all the rest are happy they escaped.' It is amusing that Thornton, when he does touch on one of the disasters of the retreat from Burgos, gives no hint that it was entirely the victim's own fault. Lord Dalhousie lost his baggage because he disobeyed orders and led his men into an impasse from which an angry Wellington had to rescue him.

Daily life with Wellington's army,
from J.H. Pyne's *Camp Scenes*, 1803.

It was the same thing after the glorious battle of Vittoria. Thornton perpetrates a mighty euphemism when he says that he saw on the battlefield 'a few broken carriages of different descriptions ... as the principal part of the enemy's loss *had been cleared away before we passed*' (my italics). In fact, Wellington's army had indulged in the most notorious orgy of looting of the whole war! Their trophies included millions of dollars, sacks of loaves, sheets, dresses, jewels and a large silver *pot de chambre* from King Joseph Bonaparte's travelling carriage. Because the delays caused by looting and drunkenness probably prevented the army from catching Marshal Soult and so ending the war in 1813 instead of 1814, Wellington furiously denounced his soldiers as 'the scum of the earth'.

Three other points of interest emerge from Thornton's answers on the Peninsular War: the preference of Wellington for 'quarters' for himself and his men (billets or cantonments) rather than tents or bivouacs (huts of branches); Thornton's ingenious cooking ovens in camp; Wellington's hunting. Wellington once said: 'The worst house is better than the best tent', and even more so than the best bivouac. Tents were of all shapes and sizes, some holding as many as twenty soldiers apiece. Huts of course let in the rain and snow, though on the French side of the Pyrenees the British were much impressed by the neatness of the French huts, complete with lattice windows, shutters and bookshelves. In the Pyrenees British officers would sometimes set aside one tent as their 'newsroom', where they could read the papers from England and Scotland.

Thornton's earth ovens compared favourably with the men's cooking arrangements on flat stones or in heavy iron kettles, into which all the available food was crammed together and slowly boiled; much slower than the handier French tin kettles.

Hunting began seriously in 1811, when two good packs were sent out from England. It was really in order to keep fit that Wellington indulged so regularly, sporting the sky-blue and black Hatfield colours in compliment to his friend Lady Salisbury. Tom Crane the huntsman came out with the Coldstream Guards and was famous for his expertise and bright pink coat; he and some of his hounds once inadvertently crossed the border into France but were courteously returned by the French. After the war he settled down with the Fife hunt. In the Peninsula, foxes were hunted and hares; now and then a wolf or wild-cat. Wellington usually kept eight hunters and as many more chargers. He was renowned for riding at everything, including stone walls.

The short Waterloo campaign offered Thornton opportunities for culinary prowess that had been entirely absent from poverty-stricken Portugal and Spain. A dinner, ball and supper, such as Wellington gave on 8 June 1815, ten days before the battle, were a splendid affair, enhanced by the well-stocked Brussels markets. Guests were received by Wellington at the entrance of his *hôtel* and walked through an illuminated garden into the ballroom.

The battle of Waterloo itself is given new vividness by Thornton's recollections, however much they may be 'fringe' contributions. He was not with Wellington at Quatre Bras. (Did he mount the Brussels' walls and listen

Overleaf:
A contemporary engraving of Napoleon's final defeat at the battle of Waterloo.

Kitty Pakenham, 1st Duchess of Wellington. She married the Duke (then Sir Arthur Wellesley) in 1806 when she was thirty-four years old, and this portrait by J. Slater shows her after five years of marriage and the birth of her two sons.

with the populace to the guns?). After the retreat from Quatre Bras, Wellington dined at the *Roi d'Espagne* inn on the road to Waterloo. At 4am, however, on the great day itself, 18 June, Thornton was alerted in Brussels: he must be ready to enter Wellington's HQ at Waterloo and cook the Commander-in-Chief 'a hot dinner'. To me there is something curiously touching about this order for 'a hot dinner' after Waterloo.... How nice it would have been to order a hot dinner after Hastings or Bosworth Field. But King Harold and King Richard were dead as Alava's cold mutton, whereas the Duke *knew* he would survive – hungry. 'The Finger of Providence' was upon him. It is news to me that Wellington's grim, silent, hot dinner took place in a first-floor room. He must have put the dying Gordon into his bed in the downstairs dining-room and then dined in his bedroom instead. I had always imagined that dinner on the ground floor; but I prefer the idea of an upper room for that sad 'last supper'.

The severance of the connection between James Thornton and the Duke and Duchess of Wellington was also sad in its own way. By 1820 at the latest Thornton had been promoted to the position of steward at Apsley House, the Duke's town house known as 'No. 1 London'. Unfortunately Thornton appears to have suffered from *folie de grandeur*, for he continued to cook as if for an army when only a dozen or so persons were sitting down to dinner. On 9 November 1820 the Duchess was forced to expostulate by letter. The Duke's family still possess the draft:

> I have received the bills and the letter in which they were enclosed. I have then examined the Bills now that I have the number of the company dining at Apsley House and must say the

> quantity of provisions for the number of persons is really extravagant. At the highest, the numbers were 13 persons each day for three days and of Butchers meat not including Lamb, Calves feet or Sweetbread was 298 pounds above 9 pounds to each person besides every other provision of every kind and in great quantities, of Fish (even on those days when there was no company) of Fowls, of everything! It is totally impossible, Thornton, such quantities should be necessary, although a joint of Butchers meat should be placed on the Side Table instead of the Dining Table. What you observe of Dinners at Taverns is perfectly applicable to Dinners at home. In every family in England where dinners are given those made Dishes which are but little touched at one Dinner are served up again to a different Party while but one day intervenes between the Dinners. This I know to be the case, & that for that reason many noblemen give two dinners immediately following because these two Dinners . . .

At this point the Duchess's draft letter broke off, and so did Thornton's stewardship, on 29 December 1820. He gave notice on that date. No doubt Thornton was happier at Portsmouth cooking at a Service establishment, where 2⅓ pounds of meat per head per day would probably not seem excessive. (In the Peninsula, however, the ration had been only one pound of meat per head per day. But the system used in the Peninsula of board wages augmented by scraps from the lord's table may well have encouraged Thornton to order greatly in excess of his employer's needs.)

It is tempting to suppose that among the Lieutenant-Governor of Portsmouth's guests for whom Thornton cooked was the eccentric John, 3rd Earl of Portsmouth. Lord Byron had attended his wedding in 1814 to Mary Anne Hanson, his second wife and one of his agent's two daughters. It was celebrated on a foggy morning and the

bride wore such a thick veil that (according to family legend) Lord Portsmouth was tricked into marrying the wrong sister. She took a lover and had two illegitimate children by him. The marriage was annulled, a charge of insanity being brought against the Earl. Byron, however, testified to his friend's sanity at least on the wedding day. He did not seem, remembered Byron, 'more insane than any other person going to be married'. Portsmouth died in 1853, two years after Thornton's answers to the questionnaire.

Meanwhile Wellington's peacetime domestic staff continued to make trouble. One had given a vast servants' 'Waterloo Ball' on the anniversary of the battle, another was a drunkard and a third a scandalmonger. At last the ducal household acquired an efficient and faithful housekeeper, Mrs Apostles. It was she who organized the

Overleaf:

James Thornton's letter of resignation to the Duchess of Wellington.

Misc.
Servants

Her Grace the Duchess
of Wellington

200 " –
175 " 6 " 3½
24 " 13 " 8½

Circumstances have Combined
to Make me wish to
Decline the Honor of Serving
Your Grace and the Duke
as Soon as You Can
Conveniently Allow me –

With the greatest Respect
I Remain Your Graces
Obedient Servant
J Thornton

to Her Grace
the Duchess
of Wellington
&c &c

Hatfield
Dec 29. 1810

Camp scene, an early nineteenth-century etching.

dinner for the royal visit of Queen Victoria to Stratfield Saye in 1845. The Queen was much amused when her beloved Duke piled her plate high with pudding and tarts all mixed together. The Duke was by then seventy-six years old and the old man's memory may have strayed happily back to the Peninsular War and the rough-and-ready way they used to serve food in the good old days.

Soon after the Great Duke's death there was an entertaining sequel to Fitzclarence's interview with his cook. A letter signed James Thornton appeared in *The Times* which Thornton said Fitzclarence had encouraged him to write:

> Having seen in your widely circulated paper that the late and ever-to-be-honoured Duke of Wellington had a French cook at Waterloo who is reported to have said, 'He knew the Duke would return to his dinner', I beg most respectfully to inform you that his Grace had no French cook during the campaign of Waterloo, but that I cooked his dinner on the day. . . . I may be permitted to state that his Grace rode up after the battle, and on getting off his horse Copenhagen he saw me and said, 'Is that you? Get dinner.'

Lord Frederick Fitzclarence's interview of James Thornton

MR. JAMES THORNTON, formerly Cook to the Great Duke of Wellington, lived with me nearly five years, during my command as Lt. Gvn. of Portsmouth. I can not give him *too* good a character –

During the winter of 51.52 at Medina, feeling everything connected with the habits & customs of the great Hero would be interesting to the world, particularly to Military men, I wrote out the following questions for Mr. Thornton who was pleased to answer them as will be seen, fully.

It will be observed Mr. T. cooked the Duke's dinner on the days of all his great actions from Salamanca to *Waterloo*, the Duke ordering dinner to be served on coming into his quarters at Waterloo – The received idea of the Duke's having a French cook at Waterloo is *erroneous*.

A British corporal billeted during the Peninsular Campaign,
from an engraving by Thomas Rowlandson, 1812.

When and where were you born?	On the 15th. of March 1787, at No. 21 Bryanston Street, Portman Square in the parish of Saint Marylebone, London.
Where were you educated?	At a day school in the parish in which I was born.
Where were you apprenticed?	1st. To Mr. Farrance, Cook and confectioner, at the corner of Spring Gardens and Charing Cross. 2nd. To Mr. Escudier, Hotel Keeper in Oxford Street, London.
Did you take any body as Assistant?	The son of the Earl of Enniskillen's Cook.
Who engaged for the service of the Duke of Wellington?	Sir Colin (then Major) Campbell on the 20th. of August 1811.
How did you go out to join His Grace, in what Ship, and where did you embark?	In an Hospital ship from Portsmouth, on the 5th. of September 1811.

Where did you land, and to whom did you report yourself on your arrival?	At Lisbon. Reported myself to the Commandant (but I forget his name) about the 21st. Sept. 1811[1].
Where did you join the Duke?	At Frenada[2], on the frontier of Spain.
How did you go up the Country, and who gave you Orders?	With a Detachment of the 16th. Light Dragoons, under the Command of Capt. Mackintosh, rode on a Trooper's horse. The Commandant of Lisbon.
What length was the March?	About 20 miles per day.
Who provided you with quarters, and when did you leave Lisbon?	Capt. Mackintosh got me quarters, each night when he got his own. Left Lisbon about the first week in October 1811, as nearly as I can recollect.
What struck you most on the March?	All the Villages we stopped at were in a most desolate state.

Did you see any devastation caused by the French?	No windows, scarcely any doors, and in many places the flooring of the rooms torn up to make fires for the French as they passed.
Were the Portuguese Civil?	The Portuguese were very civil, they were so wretchedly poor, that they were glad to see any person who had a shilling to spend or a penny to give.
Did they know you were the Duke's Cook?	I do not think they knew I was the Duke's cook, as I was under the protection and orders of Captain Mackintosh.
How did your Assistant travel?	My assistant rode on a Trooper's horse.
Who was at the head of this establishment?	Mr. Abordian, the Duke's Butler and Valet.
Where did you actually see the Duke first?	At Frenada, on the evening of my arrival, when the Duke returned from hunting.

Who and what people had you under your orders, during the time you were in the Peninsular?	The lad I took out with me, and a Portuguese as a scullery man.
What were the usual customs at Head Quarters, Breakfast, Lunch, and Dinner, during Winter Quarter?	During the Winter Quarter the Breakfast was from about 9 to 10 o'Clock, and the dinner at 6. No regular luncheons.
How many, breakfasted, lunched, and dined – their names and hours of the above?	The names as far as I can recollect were, The Duke, Lord F. Somerset, Major Gordon, Major Burgh, Capt. Canning, Major Campbell, Lord March, Capt. Freemantle[3], General Alava, and a Portuguese Secty, whose name I forget, besides which we had most days at dinner the Adjutant and Q. Master Generals.

Opposite:

Lord Fitzroy Somerset, 1st Lord Raglan. After Waterloo, where he lost an arm, Raglan became secretary to the Duke of Wellington in 1818 and on Wellington's death in 1852 succeeded him as Master-General of Ordnance. He is best known for his part in the Crimean War, where he commanded the British forces.

Mention all the details of the arrangement and management of the establishment. Had the Duke a large house to himself? Did the Aide-de-Camps lodge in it? Who gave you Orders?

The servants all had board wages[4], and the remains from the Duke's table. The Duke had always the best house in town, we stopped at, and if it were large enough, the Aide-de-Camps lodged in it, if not quarters were procured for them as near as possible – I always received my orders from Major Campbell, or in his absence, from Capt. Freemantle.

Had you any Orders to be always ready to move at the shortest notice?

I always had orders to be ready to start at the shortest notice, except during Winter Quarters.

How did you pack & carry the table furniture, Batterie de cuisine?

The tables were folded boards with hinges, the legs were separated and when put up formed a sort of tressal, and they were packed on the side of the Mule. The kitchen furniture was packed in boxes, and carried on the backs of the Mules.

Opposite:

Major-General Fremantle, one of the Duke's staff officers.

An officer's field canteen from the Peninsular War.

How many Mules had you for the purpose – who ordered them?

I was allowed three for my luggage, and three for myself and my assistant to ride one, I do not know how many the Butler had, but when the whole of the establishment was on the March, we had seldom less than eighty. Major Campbell gave orders to all the establishment.

When a move was expected who ordered you to be ready to March, what were your arrangements for it, how were you prepared for dinner on the day of the March, who conducted you to the Quarters of the Duke, or those he was to occupy?

When we were marching, the Q. Master went or sent on early each morning to the place ordered for Head Quarters, and marked the houses which each party were to occupy. The name of the town was given to me by Major Campbell and I found my way in the best manner I could.

Had you a good Mule? was it always the same?

I had a good Mule, always the same, except when he fell lame.

Baggage wagon on the march of the British army, 1807.

Who had charge of it?	A person called a Capatrice had charge of all the Mules and Muleteers – I procured provisions each day to start with the next morning.
What hour in the Winter Quarters, had the Duke to Breakfast and dinner?	From 9 to 10 the breakfast, and 6 in the evening for the dinner.
What numbers generally?	From 12 to 20.
Where did the Prince of Orange join the Duke, who was with him?	At Frenada in 1811. Mr. Johnson as an attendant, and a Baron something, who was called his tutor.
Did they always dine with the Prince? Did they live in the same house with the Duke?	Always dined at the Duke's table, but lodged separate, and Breakfasted in their own quarters.

Who was the Duke's Servant or Valet, did he accompany the Duke on horseback with bed clothes?

Mr. Abordian rode on a mule like the rest of us, the bed clothes were carried on mule's backs with the other baggage.

Do you remember the Battle of Salamanca?

I do.

Where did the Duke dine on that day, the hour, who was with him, did you see him on his return?

We left Salamanca, I think on the 22nd. of July 1812, and were ordered to go to the village of Aropiles[5], with our provisions, where we met the Duke and all his staff, I think about 1 or 2 o'Clock in the day. He immediately ordered us back about a league in the rear, where he came to us and took some refreshment with all his staff, in a farm yard on the ground – in less than half an hour he left us, and desired us to pack the things with all speed, and go to the rear, and wait for orders. We remained in a farm house till the middle of the following day, when Captain Canning came to us on the edge of the river that runs through Salamanca[6], and ordered us to advance to the

The Duke of Wellington at the battle of Salamanca, which laid open the way for his triumphant entry into Madrid three weeks later.

	town (the name of which I forget) about 5 leagues in front, where we arrived late in the evening – I did not see him that night.
Do you remember his dress?	His dress was a blue frock coat, a plain cocked hat, and I think a light drab cloak.
Had he any French General Officers (prisoners) at dinner?	There was a strong Regt. of Imperial Guards taken the day after the battle of Salamanca, but I do not think any of the Officers dined with the Duke, but were marched to the rear with the prisoners on the road to Salamanca.
Do you remember entering Madrid?	I do.
How long were you there?	Three weeks.

Where did you lodge the Duke?	The Duke occupied the King's Palace, all the time we were in Madrid.
Were you well received by the people?	The people received the Duke with the greatest satisfaction, cheering him, and calling him the Savior and King, some of them went so far as to Kiss his horse, and his cloak, and I believe even his boots.
Did the Duke give a Ball or large dinners?	The Duke gave two Balls while we were there, and large dinners nearly every day.
How did you arrange during the retreat for the Duke's dinners?	On our retreat from Burgos we managed the same way we did when we advanced. The Commissary provided us with meat, and the other things we purchased where we could find them.
Who should give the place to occupy for the night?	The Q. Master General always provided us with lodgings.

The Royal Palace in Madrid, where Napoleon installed his brother Joseph as King of Spain until his deposition by Wellington in 1812.

On August 12th, 1812, Wellington entered Madrid to the tumultuous welcome of the inhabitants who had suffered under the imposed rule of Napoleon's brother, Joseph.

How early did you start?	2, 3, or 4 o'Clock in the morning, were the hours at which we usually started when on the retreat.
Did the Duke take any refreshments out with him for the day?	The Duke never took any refreshments with him, when he mounted his horse, except a crust of Bread, and perhaps a hard boiled egg in his pocket.
Had you any hard day's work during the retreat?	Never had hard work during the retreat, no more persons to dine than the Duke's establishment.
Do you remember the day when you retreated through Salamanca?	When we came to Salamanca on our retreat from Burgos, we occupied the house we had before the battle of Salamanca, and we stopped there, I think 2 or 3 nights, and then retreated to our old winter quarters at Frenada, which was our winter quarters in 1811 and 1812, and the early months of 1813.

Had you a quiet winter as regarded the enemy?	The enemy never came nearer to our winter quarters than Salamanca, which I believe was about 20 leagues off.
How used the Duke to dress, in what uniform?	The Duke always dressed in a plain Blue Frock Coat and Mixed Coloured trousers, except on Grand Review, and then in Full dressed uniform.
Did he hunt, who had charge of the hounds?	The Duke had a pack of hounds, and hunted nearly every fine day during the winter quarters. He had a huntsman of the name of Crane, who had the entire charge of his hounds, he was a private Soldier I think in one of the Regiments of the Guards. The Duke took him from there, and finding him very clever in his business, gave him his discharge, and kept him in his service a considerable time after the War was over, at his house at Stratfieldsaye. I think I should state that the Head Quarters was moved from Frenada, in the early part of the month of January 1812, across the frontier into Spain, about five leagues

The egg boiler and spoon used by the Duke of Wellington's cook throughout the Waterloo campaign.

distance, to a village called Sallegos, for the purpose of being near Ciudad Roderigo, during the operations which were then going on for laying siege to, and storming that town – I think we were there about three weeks. When Roderigo was taken and secured, we returned to Frenada, and remained there till the month of March, and then we started for Elvas in Estramadura, where we remained about a week, during which time General Hill, and General Graham, were Knighted, as Knights of the Bath. The Duke Knighted them by proxy for the Prince Regent, on which occasion there was a very large dinner and Ball given by the Duke.

Head quarters was then moved to an encampment a short distance from Badajos, which place was invested and stormed on the 6th. of April following. We remained at Badajos, two days

Overleaf:

A market in Spain, *c.* 1813. Lithograph by George Cunningham the younger, from *Views in Spain and Portugal* taken during the campaigns of the Duke of Wellington.

and then retraced our steps back in the same direction we started from but not to Frenada, but to a village in Spain about 5 or 6 leagues from Frenada, the name of which I have quite forgot, here we remained for 5 or 6 weeks, until the Troops who were slightly wounded in the two sieges were recovered. At this place His Grace used to go out hunting three times a week at 3 o'Clock in the morning. Some time in the month of June, we started from this place and then began the campaign of 1812. We were marching and counter marching from that time till October, and then commenced our retreat from Burgos, and arrived at Frenada in November, where we remained till the month of May following.

I think it was about the close of the above campaign that Sir Thomas Graham left the Peninsular, in consequence of an affliction in his eyes[7], and was succeeded by Sir Edward Paget as second in command to the Duke, but was soon after taken prisoner on the retreat from Burgos – in that retreat Lord

Dalhousie lost all his Baggage, and some of his Servants were taken prisoners.

I ought to add that during the sieges above named, Col. Ponsonby[8] of the 12th. and Col. Harvey of the 14th. Light Dragoons were at Head Quarters, acting as extra Aides-de-Camp, as their Regiments (being Cavalry) were not in requisition.

How soon were you made aware of the move of the Army in 1813?

I think we left Frenada the first week in May 1813.

Did you make any more preparations than usual?

We made no more preparation in our domestic affairs than usual, but I heard the Duke give orders for the Army to march in full fighting order three days in the week from the beginning of the year till our advance into Spain[9].

Overleaf:
The Victory of Vitoria, 1813. As well as for its strategic importance, this battle was famous for the vast amount of treasure, paintings and state papers which were found by Wellington's army after the flight of King Joseph. According to Arthur Kennedy, 'the whole wealth of Spain and the Indies seemed to be here.'

How long did you continue marching before the Battle of Vittoria?

We were marching from the early part of May (with the exception of certain rest days) till the 21st. of June, on which day the battle was fought.

How near were you to the Action?

About 3 leagues from Vittoria where we slept the night before the Battle.

When you were ordered up into the town, who ordered you up, who conducted you there, where did you lodge, at what hours did the Duke dine, how long did you remain at Vittoria, where did you go to?

An orderly Dragoon came to our village about 5 o'Clock in the afternoon, and desired us to go to Vittoria as soon as possible – We lodged in Joseph Bonaparte's house – and the Duke dined about 11 o'Clock at night – we left Vittoria the next day for Pampuluna[10].

What did you see when passing over the field of Vittoria – did you see the guns, carriages etc taken from the French, Horses, Mules etc?

I saw a few broken carriages of different descriptions, and some dead horses and mules, but the principal part of the enemy's loss had been cleared away before we passed.

A British infantryman in France, *c.* 1815.

Where were you during the time of the passing the Pyrenees, and the French rivers, Nive, Nivelle, and where were you during the time of these battles and of Pampuluna?

We were in the valley of Roncesvalles in the Pyrenees in different villages, the names of which I entirely forget, as our movements were so frequent, but we passed through Irun quite late in the year, and passed the Bidossoa river by that route. I think Pampuluna was surrounded and ultimately surrendered.

What was the first French village quarters the Duke occupied?

To the best of my recollection the first Head Quarters established in France, was St. Juan de Luz[11], at which place we were when the battles of Nive, Nivelle etc. took place.

Were the French people civil – as civil as in Spain?

The French people were civil, and seemed to receive us with a hearty welcome, but perhaps that was for the sake of our money.

Where were you during the Winter of 1813?

At St. Juan de Luz till the spring.

Where did you advance in the spring, and where to at first in 1814?

Our first March from St. Juan de Luz, was across the Adour, over a bridge of large boats[12]. We left Bayonne to our right, which was Blockaded, and we continued our March till we got to Orthes, where a battle was fought. Here the Duke got wounded in the side[13], by a shell bursting, here we remained 5 or 6 days, as the French blew up the bridge, and retreated towards Toulouse.

Do you remember the circumstances of the Campaign of 1814, Battles of Orthes & Toulouse?

After the bridge was repaired at Orthes, we continued marching till we got near Toulouse, where a desperate battle was fought on Easter Sunday the 10th. of April 1814.

Did the Duke live in quarters those days?

The Duke always lived in quarters while I had the honor of serving him except at the taking of Badajos.

Overleaf:
The battle of Orthez in the Pyrenees Campaign of 1814. The French casualties were almost double those of Wellington's army.

Wellington entering Toulouse after the battle. This supposedly impregnable city, surrounded on three sides by water, was captured by Wellington on Easter Day, 1814.

Where did he lodge in Toulouse?

A few days before, and the night of the battle, our quarters were in a village four leagues from Toulouse, on the morning after the battle we went to Toulouse, and lodged in the principal House in the Town – I think it was the Mayor's house.

How soon did your establishment break up after the battle?

The Duke remained at Toulouse, a few Balls and dinners till about the end of April, he then went to Madrid, with part of his staff. Shortly after this we (his Servants) were ordered to pack up all the baggage and take it to Burdeaux, in boats down the rivers Garronne and Gironde. We waited at Burdeaux, till the Duke returned from Madrid and shortly after that, we (his Servants) went home with the baggage in the Duncan Man of War, and the Duke and his staff went on to Paris, and from there to England.

How long were you in England, where did you go to, were you still in the Duke's service?

When the Duke went as Ambassador to Paris I left his service – While his grace was Ambassador in Paris, he kept French Cooks.

When did you go to Brussels, the month etc?

When I left the Duke's service in the autumn of 1814 I went on a job for the winter months to Sir Patrick Murray in Scotland – I returned to London in the month of April following, and was again engaged by Sir Colin Campbell, and ordered by him to go to Brussels immediately. I think it was about the middle of May when I arrived there.

Had the Duke a large staff who used to dine constantly at his table? Who were they – their names – Was the Duke come from Vienna when you first arrived at Brussels?

The Duke was there when I arrived, his staff consisted of as nearly as I can recollect Lord Fitzroy Somerset, Colonel Henry, Sir Colin Campbell, Col. Burgh, Major Canning, Col. Freemantle, Capt. Cathcart, Major Percy, Col. Gordon, and I believe some others, but I forget who they were. They all dined at the Duke's table but the Duke breakfasted alone.

Had the Duke large dinner parties at Brussels, before the battle of Waterloo, besides his staff, and those who always dined at his table?

The Duke had large dinners nearly every day and three large Balls during our stay in Brussels.

What day and hour did you first hear of the probability of a move, or action? Did the Prince of Orange dine with the Duke the day of the Duchess of Richmond's ball?

The Duke dined at home on the day of the Duchess of Richmond's ball, which was the last night he was in Brussels till after the battle, the first course was not over when the Prince of Orange came and desired to see the Duke immediately. They closeted together for some time, when Sir Colin gave us orders to be prepared to start at a moment's notice, the second course on that day was not served up.

Did the Duke dine at home the day before he left for Waterloo? What hour did the Duke leave on the morning of the 16th., had he breakfast before he started, at what hour, what orders had you for the day on the Duke's leaving – Did he ride, or go in a carriage, did you see him go, did you send any refreshments with him – how did you send them?

The Duke went to the Duchess' ball and remained there about two hours, I do not think he went to bed at all, he had his breakfast about 6 o'Clock the next morning, and at 10 left Brussels on Horse back with all his staff[14], Orderly Dragoons and one groom with led horses. I had orders from Sir Colin to send a basket of cold provisions on the afternoon of that day, by the Butler on horse back I believe it was to a place he called Genappe, the Butler took the basket away, and I heard no more of him or the Duke till the morning of the 18th – at 4 o'Clock, when the Butler came to my bed room and told me I was to go or send my Assistant to Waterloo, as the Duke wished to have a hot dinner on that day – I immediately arose and went to market, procured a quantity of

Overleaf:
The Duchess of Richmond's ball in Brussels on the eve of Waterloo, 15 June, 1815. This 'most famous ball in history' was the occasion at which Wellington received the news that Napoleon had crossed the Sambre to attack the Prussian army under Blücher. The following morning the Duke set out for the final battles of Quatre Bras and Waterloo.

provisions and packed them in baskets – the Butler did the same with some wine, Tea, Sugar etc. and he sent them off by two men to Waterloo. I then procured a horse and accompanied by the Butler arrived at Waterloo at 11 o'Clock. I cooked the dinner and the Duke came home at half past twelve o'Clock at night and dined.

Who dined the day of the battle?

The whole of the staff that were left alive, and not wounded likewise Sir Sidney Smith and Lord Apsley[15].

What Room did the Duke dine in?

In his Bed Room up stairs.

Where was Lord Fitzroy Somerset, and Col. Gordon or Canning?

Lord Fitzroy Somerset and the Prince of Orange left Waterloo, before the Duke returned, for Brussels, the former with the loss of his right arm, the latter with a wound in his breast[16] by a Musket Ball. – Col. Gordon was lying with his leg cut off in the dining room of the house, and

Col. Canning was slain in the afternoon.

You must have heard the firing all day.

I heard the firing of artillery very distinctly before I reached Waterloo, and also more or less the whole of the day.

Had you any false reports during the day?

We had false reports from about 3 o'Clock till near dark, and a number of soldiers who had lost their Regiments, and many wounded passed through Waterloo, towards Brussels.

How soon did you hear the enemy had retired?

We did not hear of the enemy's retreat for a certainty, until a short time before the Duke returned, but there were many flying reports before that time.

The Duke returned from the field about ½ past 12 o'Clock at Night, *I was standing in the entrance passage when he came in*, there were some officers in

Overleaf:
The wounding of Crown Prince William of the Netherlands. A ball shattered his left shoulder but he survived the battle to become known as one of the heroes of Waterloo.

AUSTERLITZ
JENA
WAGRAM

	the passage and the Duke said to them "how are you," and then seeing me he said, let us have dinner directly.
How soon did you know the Duke was safe and not wounded?	Not positively till he returned.
When did you hear the Prince of Orange was wounded?	I think it was about 5 o'Clock in the afternoon at the same time Col. Gordon was brought in on a door by six Artillery men with his leg taken off.
Could you distinguish any variation as to the distance of the opponents sound of the firing during the day?	Very little variation as to sound.
Was there any cessation or stop in the firing during the day?	Scarcely any cessation of firing during the day.

We ought to have more of the Cavalry between the two high Roads. That is to say three Brigades at least besides the Brigade in observation on the Right; & besides the Belgian Cavalry & the D. of Cumberland's Hussars.

One heavy & one light Brigade might remain on the left.

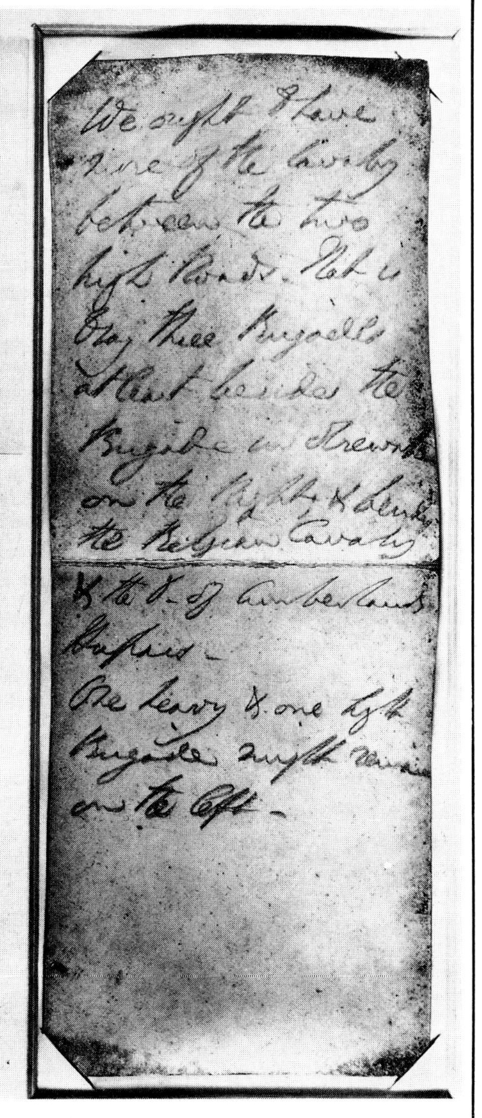

Part of the prepared hide on which Wellington wrote his orders to the unit commanders at Waterloo.

The mule box on which Wellington wrote his orders during the battle of Waterloo.

Did you hear often from the field during the action?

We received no Official information from the field during the action, but a variety of Reports, such as, the battle was lost, and the Allies on the retreat, and the vast quantity of Wounded Soldiers that came through the Village made a good many people believe it.

Where were you encamped before Badajos, what sort of Tents had the Duke, his staff, servants, Kitchens and yourself?

The Tent the Duke occupied to sleep in was enclosed in a large Marquee, the Marquee serving for sitting and dining room, the gentlemen of the staff had a tent each, smaller than the Marquee, – I had a round tent to sleep in, the Butler one also, my two Assistants had one between them, the Duke's footman and all the staff servants had one tent for two servants, all the servants' tents were round ones, the gentlemen's small Marquees – the Duke's tent was very near the others, they were all pitched in one field.

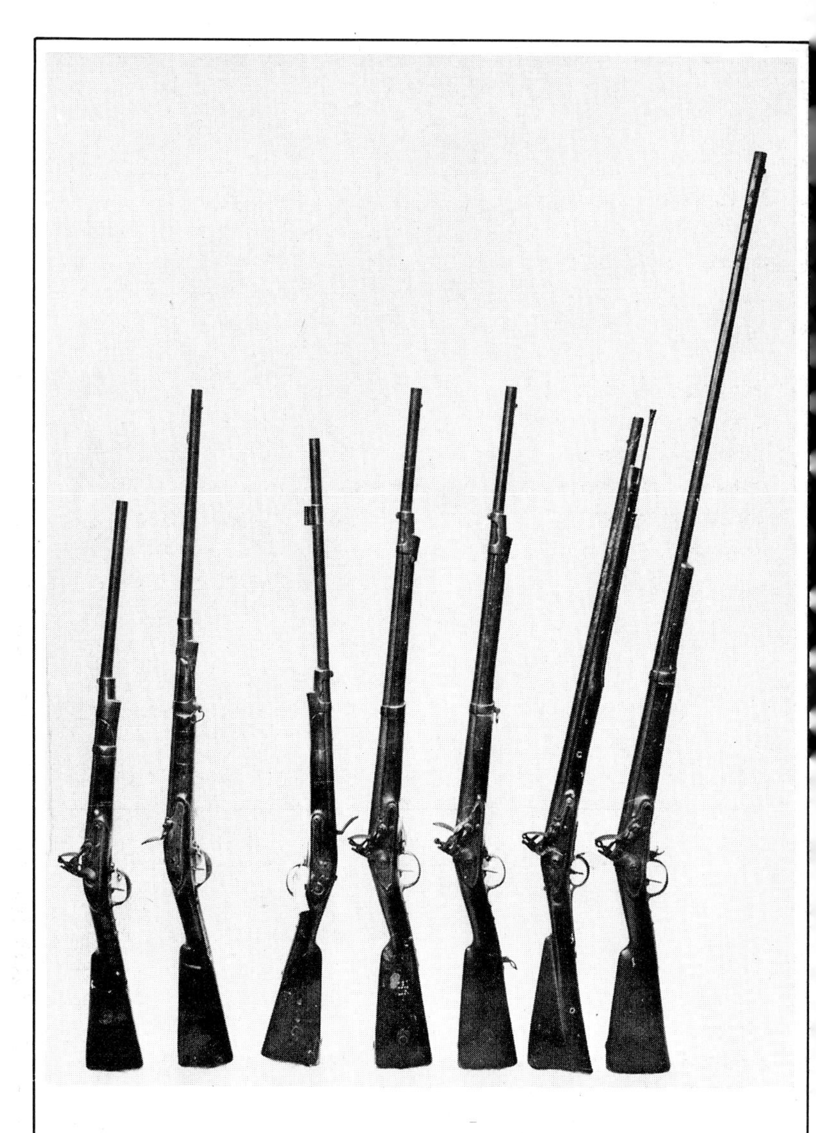

Firearms used by the French and British armies at Waterloo. From left to right: five French light cavalry carbines, a British carbine and a French musket.

How near was the Duke's tent to the nearest Regl. tents?

I cannot say how far the Regimental tents were from us, but I could see them in all directions a good distance off.

How did you cook in the camp, what fire places had you, had you smaller dinners in camp than in quarters?

I had a Room made with poles and a tarpolain, a table on trestles to prepare my dinners in. There was a mound of earth thrown up in the shape of Balloon, and niches cut round this in which we made fires and boiled the sauce pans.

We had a larger niche cut out for roasting, we stuck a pole in the top of that, and dangled the meat, when it rained hard, they had nothing but cold meat and bread. We never had any company to dinner while in camp, except the staff.

There was a sentry always placed at the entrance of the Duke's tent.

After the battle, when did you return to Brussels?

We returned to Brussels on the following morning the 19th.

N
L'EMPER
NAPOLÉ
AU
N
DÉPARTEM
DE SEIN
ET OIS
N

Napoleon's flag, presented to Wellington on the surrender of Paris in 1815.

Did the Duke dine in Brussels the following day? Who dined with him?

The Duke dined in Brussels that day with his staff, I think no other person dined there, as there was only four entrées served that day.

How long did you remain in Brussels? Where did you go to the first day on leaving it?

We left Brussels the following morning, the 20th. I cannot recollect the name of the place we stopped at the first night, in fact I recollect the names of only three places between Waterloo and Paris, they are Catteau, Malplaquet and Niville. Perronne was on our line of march but we did not stop there, it was taken from the enemy on our march to the capital, but whether by capitulation or storm, I forget, but I think the latter, as I recollect one officer telling another that the Duke had risked his life unnecessarily for so paltry a place as Perronne[17]. I think we arrived in Paris the first week in July.

How did you travel etc?

In our march from Waterloo, we had five carriages, the first was the Duke's carriage with four horses, driven by the Head coachman, the second was a carriage for the plate, with the Butler and his Assistants, driven by the second coachman. The third was a sort of carriage for the kitchen furniture, with myself and my assistants, the fourth was the old Nelson with the coachman's baggage, the fifth was the Duke's curricle, drawn by two horses, and there were two led horses ridden by the coachman's lads. These were all independant of the Saddle horses, the Duke rode on horseback all the way.

What hour did you begin your march?

We commenced our march every morning from 5 to 6 o'Clock.

Were the people civil?

The people were very civil indeed, but particularly shy, in consequence of the treatment they met with from the Prussians, who always preceeded us a day's march.

Overleaf:
British troops bivouacking in the Champs Elysées, Paris, *c.* 1815.

Did you see the Prussians or hear anything of them?

The Prussian Head Quarters of today, was our Head Quarters tomorrow, and the houses we had after them were in the most delapidated state imaginable, as they had been in the habit of taking anything they could lay hands on. It was with the greatest difficulty I could procure provisions on the road although I shewed them plenty of Dollars and told them I would pay for every thing I got!

Do you remember the Army marching into the Bois de Bologne?

I remember the Head Quarters marching into Paris, I think it was the same day that part of the British Army encamped in the Bois de Bologne[18], a great number of Troops marched into Paris the same day, the Duke amongst them. It was the most brilliant sight I ever saw in my life – I believe the greatest part of the population of Paris were in the Champs Elisee as we passed.

Do you remember Lady Caroline Lamb, breaking the Duke's bust at Paris?

Lady Caroline Lamb was a frequent guest at the Duke's house, and I have a faint recollection of a bust being broken at one of her visits, but the particulars of which I have quite forgotten[19].

Do you remember the old carriage "The Nelson"? Was it not in Spain?

I do not recollect the old Nelson carriage being in Spain, indeed I do not think it was there at all, there was only one carriage at Headquarters during the last three years of the Peninsular campaign, and there was one belonging to the Royal Family of Portugal, there were six mules for it, and it was under the charge of the Capatrice of the Mules, and I understood it was sent to Headquarters, in case any of the staff should be wounded, and not able to ride on a horse. I never saw it used but once, and that was when we marched from Frenada to Elva, for the storming of Badajos.

On the morning of leaving of Frenada, the Duke received a letter informing him of the death of the Marquis of Londonderry's (then Genl. Stewart) first wife –

he was at that time Adjutant General, and when the Duke broke the news to him, he was so much affected as not to be able to ride on horseback. The Duke then ordered the carriage to be got ready and rode in it with Genl. Stewart, the whole of that day's march. The only time I ever knew the Duke to ride in a carriage during all his campaigns[20].

Opposite:

The notorious Lady Caroline Lamb, wife of the 2nd Viscount Melbourne. Lady Caroline, a member of the aristocratic set in which Wellington moved, became famous for her turbulent love affair with the poet Byron.

Footnotes

1 The Commandant at Lisbon was Major General Warren Marmaduke Peacocke, late Captain in the 2nd Foot Guards, who received the rank of Major General on 4 June 1811.
2 Freineda.
3 Fremantle.
4 When Sir Arthur Wellesley left for Portugal the first time in 1808 he told his wife Kitty, née Pakenham, to put one of the male servants on board wages: 'George is to have 14 shillings a week Board Wages; if he should want more, or not be satisfied give him warning, for it is high time to draw a line.'
5 The village of Los Arapiles.
6 The River Tormes.
7 Graham was able to return to Spain and fight at Vittoria.
8 Colonel Frederick Ponsonby was severely wounded at Waterloo. His sister, Lady Caroline Lamb, came to Paris to visit him and make merry. Colonel Felton Hervey was to marry one of the beautiful American Caton sisters, Louisa, while her sister Marianne married, first, Edward Patterson brother of Betsy Patterson-Bonaparte, and when widowed, Wellington's brother the Marquess Wellesley.
9 This was to get into training for the great march to Vittoria.
10 Pamplona.
11 St Jean de Luz. The army loved this pretty, healthy place. Their last HQ in Spain had been Lesaca, which smelt 'like an old poultry-yard'.
12 The much praised pontoon bridge constructed by Sir John Hope.
13 Wellington's wound was caused by a spent bullet forcing his sword hilt against his thigh and breaking the skin. It was his only war wound.
14 Wellington snatched under two hours' sleep between 3 am and 5 am on the morning of 16 June and left Brussels about 8 am, reaching Quatre Bras at 10.30 am.
15 Admiral Sir Sidney Smith had retired from the navy in 1814 and

happened to find himself in Brussels in June next year. He boasted of being the first Englishman, not in the battle, to shake Wellington's hand after the victory. Generals Alava and Müffling were also present at the dinner.

16 The musket ball was in the Prince's shoulder.

17 Thornton was not mistaken in believing that it had been a toss-up between surrender and storming, but in the end the fortresses *en route* to Paris were surrendered by their governors to Wellington, in the name of Louis XVIII.

18 One of the large huts constructed from felled trees was called by the troops 'The British Hotel'.

19 Thornton was well advised to be vague about Caroline's misbehaviour. Gossip proliferated; but there is evidence that in her wild moods she did tend to break up vases and ornaments, and she once burnt Byron's portrait on a bonfire. In the Hôtel Meurice at Paris she virtually laid waste the room in which she was staying with her husband William Lamb, the future Prime Minister Lord Melbourne. Wellington regarded her as 'a little mad' but was amused by her and her 'accidents', as well as trying to reconcile her to her husband.

20 The Duke did indeed send for a carriage from England, large enough to sleep in but only for emergencies. Thornton was right in saying that he stuck to his chargers throughout the campaign, learning to sleep in the saddle as comfortably as if he were in bed. When Stewart went home, Wellington bought from him his young charger Copenhagen, foaled in 1808. Never did Wellington make a better buy. Copenhagen carried him through Waterloo, the Duke paying him a typical compliment after his death at Stratfield Saye in 1836: 'for bottom and endurance I never saw his fellow'. He was a horse fit for a hero.

Acknowledgements

The publishers would like to thank Bernard Tomlinson who owns the original manuscript and suggested it for publication.

Picture Credits
British Museum *48*
City of Bristol Museum & Art Gallery *116*
Courtauld Institute of Art *42*
By kind permission of His Grace the Duke of Wellington (photograph Eileen Tweedy) *46*
The Trustees of the Goodwood Collection *97*
National Army Museum, London *6, 15, 52, 60, 63, 79, 83, 85, 101, 106, 113*
National Portrait Gallery, London *10*
Royal Irish Fusiliers Regimental Museum *76*
Victoria & Albert Museum *13, 19, 21, 22, 25, 28, 31, 33, 41, 56, 59, 67, 73, 89, 91, 103, 104, 109*